Fancy NANCY and the Quest for the Unicorn

Based on *Fancy Nancy* written by Jane O'Connor
Cover illustration by Robin Preiss Glasser
Interior illustrations by Carolyn Bracken

HARPER FESTIVAL
An Imprint of HarperCollinsPublishers

HarperFestival is an imprint of HarperCollins Publishers.

Fancy Nancy and the Quest for the Unicorn
Text copyright © 2018 by Jane O'Connor
Illustrations copyright © 2018 by Robin Preiss Glasser
For information address HarperCollins Children's Books, a division of HarperCollins Publishers, 195 Broadway, New York, NY 10007.
www.harpercollinschildrens.com

Library of Congress Control Number: 2017962819
ISBN 978-0-06-237794-4

19 20 21 22   CWM   10 9 8
❖
First Edition

Bree and I are absolutely obsessed with unicorns. That means we are super-duper interested in them. Unicorns are mythical creatures, which means they are not real...

but they are almost real to us.

Today we're playing Quest for the Unicorn.
(Quest is a fancy word for search.)
"Please, please, can we play too?" Freddy begs.

Bree and I are both wonderful big sisters,
so we let Freddy and JoJo join us.

We all wait while my dad hides one of my toy unicorns in the backyard. "Don't make it too easy!" I shout to him.

Off we go on our quest.

Ooh la la! We spot something glittery.

Could it be the unicorn's tail?

No. It is a hair clip I lost ages ago.
Our quest is not over.

Then I shout, "Look over yonder! By the bush. Could it be a unicorn horn I spy?"

We all race over.
Alas, it is just a twisted branch.

So we all quest some more, and a little later Bree clutches my arm. "Hey, I see something, and it is pure white!"

This must be the unicorn!

But no. It is just Frenchy's new toy bunny.

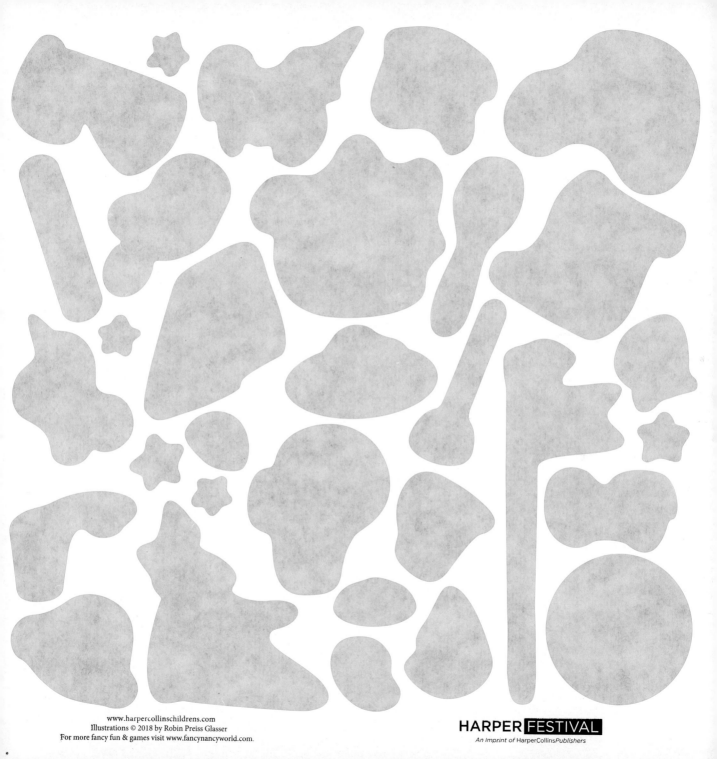

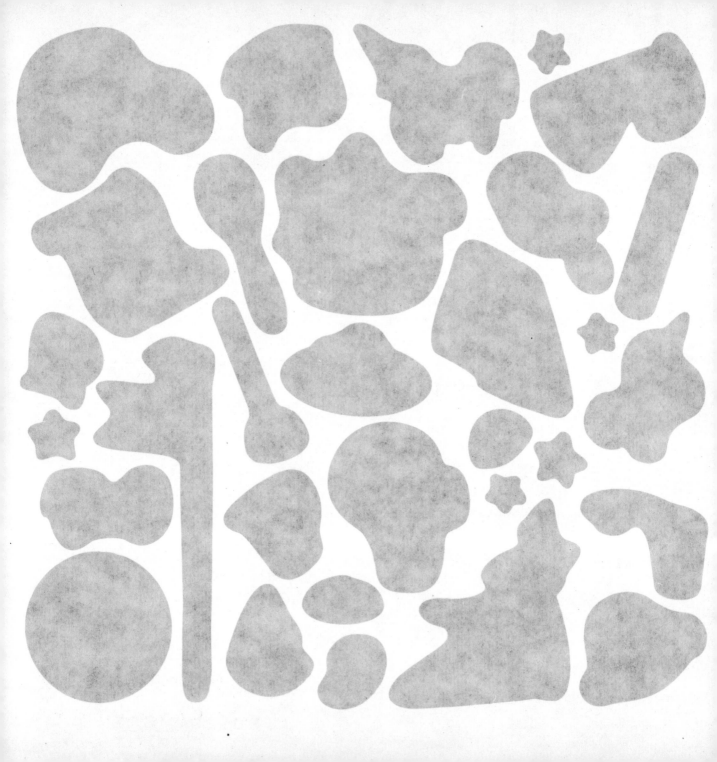

We search high and low in the backyard.
JoJo and Freddy are getting
frustrated—that's fancy for fed up.

"We're tired of questing," JoJo says.
"Fine!" I say. "Go play by yourselves.
Bree and I will continue the quest without you."

"Dad, I didn't want you to make the hiding place easy. But this is too daunting." (That's fancy for difficult.)

"Well, I'm not a unicorn expert like you fair maidens," my dad tells us. "However, I once heard that unicorns like lilacs."

Lilacs! My mom planted
lilac bushes last spring.

Voilà! In the branches is a unicorn.

Our quest is over! Now it is time for refreshments.
We head to the clubhouse.

Of course, JoJo and Freddy show up and want to join our tea party. "Please, please, please," JoJo pleads.

"Sorry. This is a questers-only tea party," I inform her.

We are nibbling cookies and sipping pink lemonade when my dad appears.

"JoJo and Freddy are sorry they were quitters," he says. "You girls are such incredible big sisters. Won't you reconsider letting them join you?"

It's true. Bree and I are wonderful big sisters. So we relent, which means we give in. A minute later we are putting out more cookies and lemonade.

And lo and behold! JoJo has a surprise!
A tiny unicorn is in her hand. They found it in the sandbox.
"I don't ever remember seeing that one," I tell them.
"You both are excellent questers after all."

I told you unicorns are mythical—
maybe they are a little bit magical too!